HOW TO PLAY TENNIS

MAVEN BOOKS

HOW TO PLAY TENNIS

P. A. Vaile

"Modern Lawn Tennis," "Great Lawn Tennis Players,"

"The Strokes and Science of Lawn Tennis,"

"The Soul of Golf," "Modern Golf," etc.

MAVEN BOOKS

Chennai   Trichy   New Delhi

MAVEN BOOKS

This edition has been published in india by arrangement with Carson Books, UK

ISBN 978-93-90877-88-1   Maxwell Press

All rights reserved   No. 44, Nallathambi Street,

India   Chennai 600 005

MJP 1024   © Publishers, 2023

Publisher's Note

The legacy of a country is in its varied cultural heritage, historical literature, developments in the field of economy and science. The top nations in the world are competing in the field of science, economy and literature. This vast legacy has to be conserved and documented so that it can be bestowed to the future generation. The knowledge of this legacy is slowly getting perished in the present generation due to lack of documentation.

Keeping this in mind, the concern with retrospective acquiring of rare books has been accented recently by the burgeoning reprint industry. MAVEN BOOKS is gratified to retrieve the rare collections with a view to bring back those books that were landmarks in their time.

In this effort, a series of rare books would be republished under the banner, "MAVEN BOOKS". The books in the reprint series have been carefully selected for their contemporary usefulness as well as their historical importance within the intellectual. We reconstruct the book with slight enhancements made for better presentation, without affecting the contents of the original edition.

Most of the works selected for republishing covers a huge range of subjects, from history to anthropology. We believe this reprint edition will be a service to the numerous researchers and practitioners active in this fascinating field. We allow readers to experience the wonder of peering into a scholarly work of the highest order and seminal significance.

MAVEN BOOKS

B. F. McManus, Photo.

P. A. VAILE

Contents

Introduction

The wonderful popularity of THE STROKES AND SCIENCE OF LAWN TENNIS has induced the American Sports Publishing Company to commission the author, Mr. P. A. Vaile, to write a more rudimentary treatise. Mr. Vaile's fame as an authority on sport is world-wide. This is his fourth book on Tennis, his other works on the game in addition to "The Strokes and Science of Lawn Tennis," being "Modern Lawn Tennis" and "Great Lawn Tennis Players." In addition to these, Mr. Vaile has also written (inter alia) "Modern Golf," "The Soul of Golf," and "Swerve or the Flight of the Ball."

Mr. Vaile's knowledge of tactics has brought him world-wide recognition and in his French translation of "Modern Lawn Tennis," Max Decugis, then champion of France, tells how he defeated A. W. Gore, then champion of England, for the championship of London, by following the tactics which Mr. Vaile had laid down for him.

The publishers are convinced that if the lessons taught by Mr. Vaile in this book and in "The Strokes and Science of Lawn Tennis" are properly learned, they will have a very great and beneficial effect on Tennis in America.

Foreword

Although this book is called "The Tennis Primer," I hope that it will prove of great use to the most expert tennis players, for few of them have a backhand drive. I have herein paid special attention to this branch of the game, for the execution of this stroke is almost a lost art, and there is no reason why it should be so if players will take the trouble to study carefully the photographs given in illustration of this very fine drive.

P. A. VAILE.

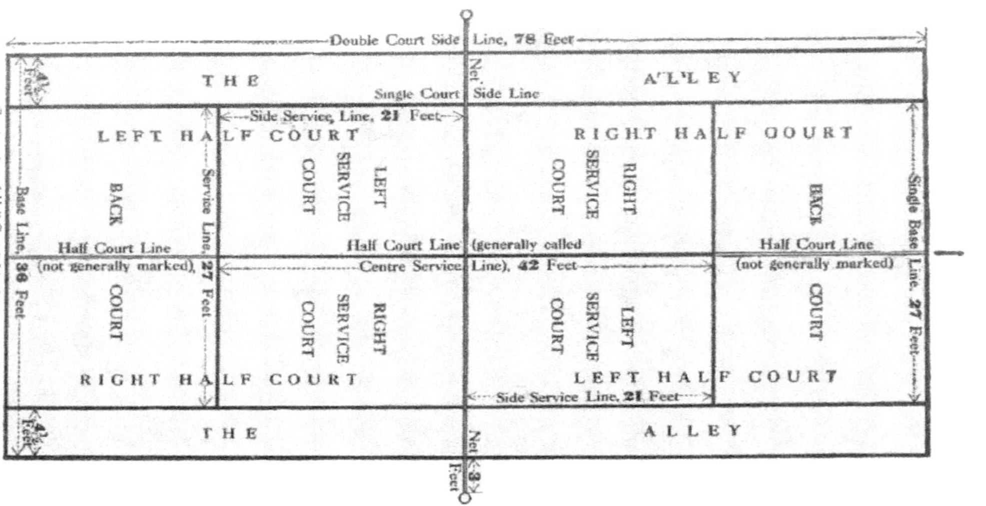

DIAGRAM OF A TENNIS COURT

Description of the Game

Tennis is played by two or four persons. When two persons play the game it is called a Single, when four, a Double. When the game is played by men it is called a Men's Single or Men's Double, as the case may·be. When by ladies, or as they say in America, women, it is called, in England, a Ladies' Double, in America, a Women's Double. When a lady and a man play a similarly constituted pair, it is called a Mixed Double.

The size of the Court for the single game is 78 feet by 27 feet. The Double Court is 78 feet by 36 feet.

The game is played with rackets, or, as they are sometimes called bats, and balls, and it consists of a series of "rests," or "rallies." A "rest" signifies the number of times a ball has been played backwards and forwards consecutively over the net. That is to say, a rest consists of the play which ensues from the time a good service leaves the racket of the server until the ball is dead.

A net runs across the court in the middle, parallel with the base lines and dividing the court into two equal spaces. The ball is played from one side of this net to the other until one of the players fails to return it into the opponent's court. Either side scores a point when the opposing side fails to return the ball into the opponent's court.

This point may be obtained by one's opponent failing to hit the ball, by hitting it into the net, or by the ball falling out of the opponent's court. The object of the game of Tennis is, therefore, to place or drive the ball into the

Plate 1.

THE GRIP OF THE RACKET.

The best way to learn the forehand grip is to lay the racket on the table as shown in Plate 1. Then proceed as shown in following plates.

opponent's court in such a manner as to prevent him from returning it into one's own court.

The person who puts the ball in play is called the Server. He throws the ball up as specified and hits it across the net into the service court diagonally opposite.

After the Server has done this each side must strike the ball alternately, hitting it before it touches the ground, in which case the stroke is called a "volley," or, if it has struck the ground, a "ground stroke."

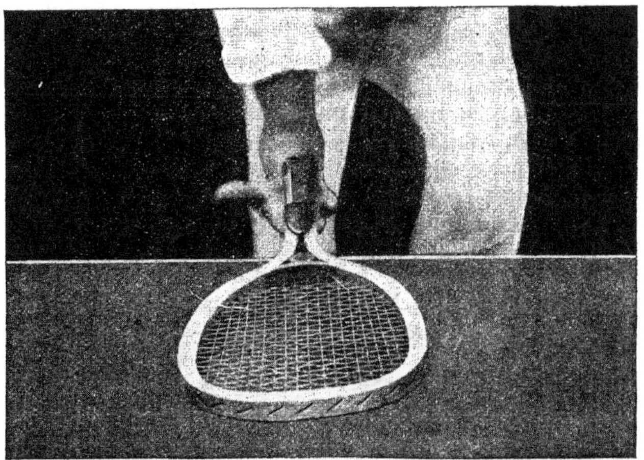

Plate 2.

FOREHAND GRIP.

Open the hand. Place it under the racket handle, as shown, so that the handle of the racket and the forearm are in the same line.

It must be remembered that one must not volley the service; that is to say, the service must not be struck before it touches the ground. The player who does this loses the stroke. All balls other than the service may be either volleyed or played off the ground.

The first point, or ace, won by either side is called 15-love and if each side wins one of the first two points it is called "15-all."

The server's score is always called first, so that the score

Plate 3.

FOREHAND GRIP.

Now let the hand turn sufficiently to the side, as shown in Plate 3, to grip the racket.

would in the foregoing case be called "15-love" or "love-15" and "15-all," according to whether the server or his opponent wins the first stroke. "Love," in tennis scoring, means nothing.

If the server wins the first two strokes, the score is

"30-love." If his opponent wins the next one it is "30-15."
If the server loses the next one the game is "30-all."

It will thus be seen that the first two strokes are given
a value of 15 each. The third stroke is assessed at 10, so

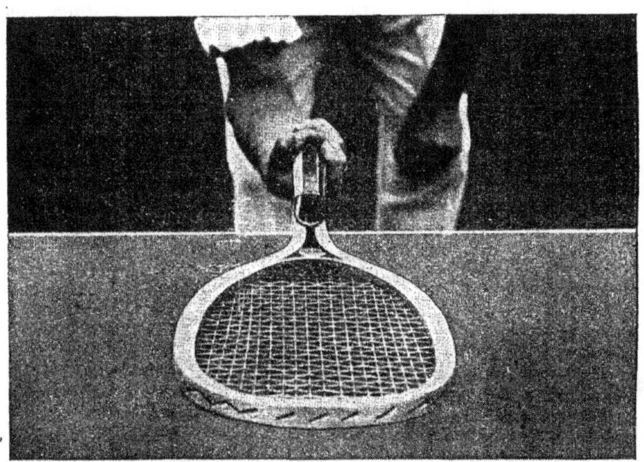

Plate 4.

FOREHAND GRIP.

Close the hand round the racket. This gives the proper forehand grip used by the greatest players of modern times, and also
of those who made the history of the game before the present
unsound English grip was introduced.

that if "30-all" has been called and the server wins the
next point the score is called 40-30. Should the receiver,
or striker-out, as he is generally called, win the next point
after "30-all," the score would be called 30-40.

A game is won by either side when four aces or points have been scored, unless each side wins three points, which means "40-all," but is always called "Deuce."

At Deuce it is necessary for either side to win two consecutive strokes before the game is won, so that once the

Plate 5.

FRONT VIEW OF FOREHAND GRIP.

Notice that the arm and handle are in the same line. This is most important. Notice also that the leather is *in* the hand, which is unusual now. It is, however, the old grip, and forehand or backhand, is still probably the best.

score has gone to deuce neither side can win by the result of one "rest."

If, when the score is deuce, the server wins the next ace, it is " 'vantage in." Should he then win the next,

the game is his, but should he lose it the game goes back
to deuce and both he and his opponent require to score
two consecutive strokes before the game is won, so that if
the score is " 'vantage in," the receiver must score three
successive strokes to win. He wants one to bring it back

Plate 6.

THE BACKHAND GRIP.

The principle of the arm and racket handle being in the same
line, or at least in the same plane of force is well exemplified here.

to deuce, a second to take it to a " 'vantage out," and the
third for "game."

After the first game is won the receiver becomes the
server, and so on alternately. The score is always called
with the server's score first. When the games are equal

they are called "1-all," "2-all," "3-all," and so on, but if it is "5-all," either side must win two games in succession before the set is won. The games in scoring are not called "deuce" or " 'vantage"; "5-all," or "6-5," would be called, but the same rules apply as in the case of deuce or 'vantage

Plate 7.

ALTERNATIVE BACKHAND GRIP.

Many players put the thumb up the back of the handle for the backhand stroke. I always do when driving, but not so habitually when volleying. It is not necessary, but I believe it aids direction.

in the game; for instance, if the score is 5-6 in a set, the server would require to win one game to bring the score to 6-all, and then he would have to win two more games, consecutively, before the set would go to him.

There is no fixed rule as to what constitutes a match. Any club or tournament committee may settle the point for themselves. Matches are, however, usually the best two of three sets.

Men's championship matches are generally decided on

Plate 8.

FRONT VIEW OF BACKHAND GRIP.

This shows how the racket appears from the front. Notice the arm and handle in the same plane and the leather at the end of the handle *in* the hand. This allows much greater freedom of wrist action than if the end of the racket protrudes.

the best of five sets. The side which shows 3-2, 3-1 or 3-love, in sets, winning.

Matches in which women play are always decided by the best of three sets.

The ball in service must never be volleyed, that is, hit before it strikes the ground; but the receiver must wait until the ball has hit the ground before he can strike it.

The game is played on a variety of courts—grass, sand, dirt, asphalt, cement, wood and others—but there is no court so suitable for the game as grass.

Great care should be taken in laying out a court to allow plenty of room all around it.

I have designedly dropped the prefix "lawn" in dealing with the game. The time has come for it to take its proper place and leave the older game, which is comparatively unknown, to adopt some distinctive title.

How to Make and Keep a Court

I have laid out a considerable number of grass courts and my advice to any one who wants to do the same thing is to get some person who makes it his business to do it for him if he can afford it. If he cannot, or if he wants the work and "fun," I must try to help him. I have already given the plan and dimensions of the single and double courts, so I shall address myself here merely to the question of construction.

These are general instructions, and must, of course, in many cases, be subject to local conditions. See that the site which you select is protected from the prevailing winds, if you can conveniently arrange it so by taking advantage of any natural shelter, but on no account have any trees, particularly deciduous trees, near it.

Having selected your site, you must lay down your side line and measure out your court. Now comes the important matter of settling your levels, and I don't mind telling you that I generally employed a surveyor to do it for me. If you cannot get a surveyor you can manage it for yourself by driving in a stake or two with a straight-edge nailed on at a right angle, putting a spirit-level on that, and repeating the operation with the other stakes. You will have to level from·stake to stake by another straight-edge and level, which I am afraid you will find rather tedious.

Plate 9.

THE SERVICE.

It is advisable to hold two balls in the hand when serving. Later one may hold more if desired. Practically, more than two tend to interfere with accuracy of placing the ball in the air for the delivery of the service. The racket starts low down so as to get momentum for the stroke.

You must endeavor to lay out your court so that the sun will pass as nearly as may be across it in the same line as the net.

Having got your levels, the next thing will be to reduce the ground. If you are adding the soil to make the lawn, you will simply have to straighten out the ground roughly and spread your soil on top. You must be careful to get good soil free from weeds.

If you are using the soil already there, you must, if your excavation would take you into poor soil, lay back the good soil on each side, level up the subsoil and spread the good soil again. You must then see that it is thoroughly pulverized and raked, and every sign of a weed must be taken out. When you have gone thoroughly over it, and raked it until there is not a nut or a weed in it, you may sow it. Here I must leave you to the tender mercies of your seedsman with the warning to avoid clover as you would sin, and to use nothing but fine lawn grasses suitable for your district and climate.

In sowing you must be careful to spread the seed well with a free circular sweep of the hand, which releases the seed equally at all portions of its passage; in fact, unless you know how to do it, again you had better get some one who does. Whatever you do, be generous with the seed. Put on 50 per cent more than the seedsman tells you to rather than 10 per cent less. You should sow when the

Plate 10.

SERVING.

Note carefully weight mainly on right foot, now shifting to left;
feet almost at right angle, right ankle and knee bent to give the
snap; left arm and shoulder high up, right arm and shoulder low
down (as in cricket or base ball when delivering the ball) while
the body is bent back a little from the waist.

ground is dry, then roll well with an ordinary roller. You can run a brush or bough over the lawn so as to sweep all seeds into the soil, or rake lightly again. Then roll once more, and Nature will do the rest.

This is really a very general direction, but it is hard to be more specific, as the conditions in each case vary so much; but whatever you do take no notice of the local quidnunc who advises you to have clover because it is always so nice and green, like the balls will be and he is, or some other kind of grass because it is so soft, as he apparently thinks you are.

You may, of course, want to turf your lawn. Good turf is in many places quite impossible to get. We will assume, however, that you can get it and that you have levelled out your lawn and the surrounding ground. You must be careful to see that it is well drained. In some cases it will be right without anything further. In others you will have to tile-drain it. Here again I am afraid you will want the tradesman, as so few amateurs can do this properly.

. You should have at least ten inches of good soil above the sub-soil before you think of putting down your turf, and it stands to reason that this must be perfectly and equally consolidated all over, otherwise you will have trouble with your turf. See that all your turf is of an even thickness. After the turf is laid it has to be well trodden or rammed and then lightly rolled. You must

Plate 11.

FOREHAND DRIVE WITH LIFT.

This shows the swing back for this stroke. The weight is mainly
on the right foot.

now leave it alone for a while to settle, and then in a few weeks, when it has "gripped" the soil, you may put a heavier roller on to it. During the first two or three weeks, if there is not much rain, you should have the sprayer going on the lawn.

Always keep the grass closely mown. If you allow it to grow long it becomes rank and thick at the roots, and this spoils a lawn. You can hardly cut a tennis lawn too close. I can remember nearly getting into trouble with a very worthy secretary of my club, who thought half an inch of grass made it "nice and soft for the feet," by making him an offer for the "grazing" on the lawns. He could not understand that you cannot cut a lawn too closely unless you scrape the earth up.

Shortly after the end of your season it is well to give the base lines some attention. Possibly they will want top-dressing and re-sowing, or they will perhaps, in the case of the turfed lawn, want re-turfing. In the case of a lawn where the seed has been grown on it, especially in its first year, it is a good plan to give it a top-dressing of an inch or so of good soil similar to that which was used in putting it down and to treat this with a liberal application of some of the superphosphate or bone manures so liberally advertised nowadays.

Water your court in the cool of the evening, never in the heat of the day. Keep the roller and the mower going.

Plate 12.

FINISH OF FOREHAND DRIVE WITH LIFT.

Note carefully how the forearm and racket have turned over.
This turn, however, does not take place until *after* the ball has
been struck.

These are the three chief factors in obtaining and keeping a good surface after you have once got over the initial difficulties. Carefully remove all weeds as soon as they make their appearance.

Hard Courts.—There are so many different kinds of hard courts that I cannot attempt fully to describe each one. I shall therefore give general directions which are really applicable to nearly all hard courts except such as asphalt, cement, or concrete.

For practically all hard courts the following directions will be found to answer: Excavate the soil for a depth of eight inches over the area which you intend to put down. Level the surface. Lay down about five or six inches of large gravel, broken brick, or any other stone or cinder which you care to use as a foundation. Every stone in this should be of such a size that it will pass through a two-inch ring. Have this thoroughly raked and levelled. Then roll it with a heavy roller—the heavier the better. Two and a half tons is not too heavy if your sub-soil will stand it. Roll it thoroughly, and do not water it. This will put it down very considerably.

Now put down an inch and a half to two inches of gravel, cinder, burnt clay, or whatever you are using, that is about half the size of the foundation. Have this spread a shovelful at a time and sown with a good semi-circular sweep of the shovel, so as to distribute it evenly.

Plate 13.

FOREHAND CUT DRIVE.

The racket in this case passes rapidly across the ball from right
to left.   It is the natural stroke to play on a low ball.

Sweep it well into the interstices between the large stones. Do this thoroughly. Then have it raked and smoothed and dry-roll it heavily and well.

Now you have a very solid bed, and you must start to put on your top. Let this consist of very small gravel, cinder, or stone chips. They must be small enough to readily sweep in between the interstices in the last layer and present a smooth surface. "Sow" this as before. Sweep it well in as it is put down. Give it a good dressing, and now put your water on. Don't flood it, but give it a good drenching all over, so as to wash the chips down between the larger stones. Now for the first time you wet-roll it, and you can hardly give it too much.

You ought now to have a good surface, but if you are not thoroughly satisfied with it you must, when it has dried and set, give it another dressing of smaller chips that are almost dust. Sweep these well in and water them copiously. Then roll again as heavily as you like. If you are making a sand court, your last layer would consist of, say, an inch and a half to two inches of sand, but it would then be well to have some lime or some similar substance to mix with it, otherwise it will probably not bind well unless it is fairly coarse.

You must not make the mistake of putting down too much dust on the court Your final dressing should be small chips in preference to dust, for if your last layer is

Plate 14.

FOREHAND CUT DRIVE.

A little later in the same stroke. Note the racket already beginning to turn, also the grip, which allows the greatest possible freedom for the wrist.

too fine it merely sinks between the larger stones or rubble and is in dry weather a cushion of dust and in wet a pad of mud, so that your court will not consolidate at all, and it will be as great a failure as a court as was the Thames Embankment as a road until it was paved.

In each layer you must see that you have your stones carefully graded. They should be as nearly as possible of uniform size. It is a good idea to have your court several inches higher down the centre than at the sides. This allows the water to run off freely.

Unless your site is naturally fairly well drained you should tile-drain it before you put down your foundations, or if you do not you can make your "floor" slope to some given point and put in a few pipes to carry off any soakage.

These are necessarily very general directions, but the principles are sound and will be found to answer here if intelligently carried out, even as they do in road-making, for that is what they amount to. They are practically the scientific method of road-making which is so generally neglected throughout England.

Plate 15.

FINISH OF FOREHAND CUT DRIVE.

Note here that the forearm and racket have not turned over as in the forehand lifting drive. The tendency is quite in the other direction. This return, especially from left back court to left back court produces a low swerving ball with an ugly break.

Implements and Dress

Do not get a cheap racket. Most cheap rackets are in the long run very expensive. If you do not understand how to choose a racket yourself, you should endeavor to get someone who does know. A man should use a racket from 14 to 14½ ounces. For ladies 13 ounces is right.

I am a great believer in knickerbockers for all athletic games and in the Southern hemisphere they are used by some players. The climatic conditions in the Northern hemisphere make it almost impossible to use them with comfort. No athletic game can be played to the best advantage in trousers, because they bind at the knee. Can we, for instance, imagine a base ball team playing base ball in trousers? But there can be little doubt that trousers are most convenient and comfortable, although by no means the most suitable for tennis.

It is of great importance that one should be lightly and tightly shod. One should not, of course, have one's shoes so tight as to cause inconvenience, but it is impossible to start quickly in loose shoes and it is a point of considerable importance to have the least possible weight to carry about on one's feet. A lady player should have the skirt so short and light that it does not impede her progress on the court. Hard courts require a heavier shoe than is needed for grass.

Plate 16.

THE BACKHAND DRIVE.

Plate 16 shows the beginning of the stroke, which is most important. *It starts at the elbow.* The following series of pictures is the most complete explanation of the backhand drive that has ever been given.

The Grip of the Racket

A proper grip of the racket is of the utmost importance to the game; in fact, it may be said to be the foundation of the game.

There is one outstanding principle which one must absolutely bear in mind in connection with the grip of the racket, and that is, at the time of striking the ball, the forearm and the handle of the racket must be in one and the same straight line. That is to say, if the forearm were continued in a line, it would run straight on to the handle of the racket. In many cases, the whole of the arm, from the shoulder, and the racket are in the same line or plane. This is particularly so in the backhand stroke.

There are of course many cases where the racket and the forearm are not in the same line, but when this is so, as in some portions of the backhand stroke, the arm and the racket handle are moving in the same direction, or, to put it more accurately, in the same plane.

It is impossible to exaggerate the importance of this fundamental principle. In England it is customary to play with the hand much more toward the side of the handle than is usual in America. The moment this is done one sacrifices power and direction.

If one desires to push a person forward, one would

Plate 17.

THE BACKHAND DRIVE.

This plate shows very clearly the elbow movement which takes
the racket back. Note that the weight is on the left leg.

naturally go behind him to do so. It is exactly the same with the racket. We desire to propel the ball with the racket, therefore we must be behind the racket to get the best result.

This is true of every stroke in the game and, when I say we must be behind the racket, it must be understood that I speak principally of the position of the hand on the racket handle, although as a matter of fact, in nearly every stroke in tennis the player is behind the ball, so far as regards the distance from the opponent.

Plate 18.

THE BACKHAND DRIVE.

A back view showing weight on left leg and the manner in which the racket swings back in the backhand drive.

The Game

It is important to remember that one must keep one's eye on the ball until one has hit it, and one should try to hit the ball absolutely in the centre of the racket—if one may use the term "centre" of the racket.

It is very important not to get too near to the ball, either in the line of its flight and bound or laterally.

A beginner should start by letting the ball bound so that it will fall to the second bound about two feet or two feet six inches to the right of the left foot; then he can hit it shortly before it would strike the ground the second time if he did not play it. This is the fundamental ground stroke in tennis. Of course the whole theory of modern tennis is to attack the ball at or before the top of the bound, but the fundamental ground stroke in tennis is to get the ball on the racket with the racket face upwards, so that the ball bounds off the racket as it would off a table, placed at an angle of say 40 degrees. This is the stroke which gives the player the lob and from it come the other strokes in the game.

One thing which is of the utmost importance to remember is, that at the time of making every stroke the racket should be held very firmly.

Playing with a loose wrist is one of the commonest

Plate 19.

THE BACKHAND DRIVE.

This plate shows the racket coming forward on to the ball, also
the weight being transferred to the right leg.

errors in tennis. There is no stroke in tennis which may be played with a loose wrist. All the delicacy and finesse which is shown in the game, although it is ascribed to the wrist, really comes from the turn of the forearm, the wrist being, in practically all cases, fairly rigid, and in many as firm as if cast in steel.

Between the strokes, the player will, of course, relax his hold of the racket, so as not unduly to strain his muscles, and he will when waiting for the service naturally carry the racket in both hands supporting it at the splice with his left hand.

It is important in tennis to swing well back before one hits the ball and also to follow well through after the ball, transferring one's weight, in the act of striking the ball, on the forehand from the right foot to the left in the case of the right-handed player and reversely in the case of the left-handed player.

Plate 20.

THE BACKHAND DRIVE.

A side view showing how far in front of the player the backhand
stroke is played as compared with the forehand. This position
in photographs always looks constrained. The stroke really is the
most graceful in the game, and, as in the cinematograph pictures
of a galloping horse, the individual positions are not discernible.
Note carefully the position of elbow, wrist, feet, and the bend
of the body which gives room for a full swing of the racket.

The Service

The service is used to put the ball into play, and nowadays it occupies a totally disproportionate place in the game, so much so indeed that I should not be surprised to see the service court shortened from six inches to a foot, or the service rule radically altered.

The player must get out of his mind any idea whatever that he can play tennis with one grip. There are many grips in tennis, each one to be used in its own particular place, but the same principle runs right through every grip.

The racket must be held in a straight line with the forearm or in the same plane of force with it at the moment the blow is being struck.

Nearly every beginner tries to hit the service down into the service court. This is a great mistake. There is no necessity to try to hit the service downward. It will come down of its own accord if it be hit straight away.

The beginner should make his fault over the service line. He should not put the ball into the net; there is no necessity to do so. He should send the ball a foot above the net sooner than put it into it.

In starting the service, the weight should be on the right leg. The ball is thrown up well over the right ear and struck the moment it comes within reach of the centre of the racket. As one is hitting it one's weight is shifted to the left foot and the racket is allowed to swing out after the ball until it finishes almost touching the ground.

Plate 21.

THE BACKHAND DRIVE.

This plate shows an important position. The forearm and racket
are turning over and the thumb is beginning to show at the side
of the racket as it will do if the stroke is played naturally and
the arm is allowed to follow through without constraint. Unless
the finish is made in this manner the ball will lack that invaluable
quality top-spin, for the stroke will not have been properly played.

The Forehand Stroke

The forehand stroke is the foundation of the game. No one without a good forehand stroke can be really a great player. Many players have become famous with practically nothing else than a good forehand drive, therefore it is of great importance to a player to endeavor to cultivate a good forehand.

I have spoken already of the foundation stroke in tennis. Here one almost allows the ball to reach the ground on the second bound and then tosses it up, and it will not be long before the beginner will see that he wants something better than this stroke.

It is then that he comes to the real forehand drive. This stroke is played by bringing the racket up behind the ball and striking it an upward blow which can best be described as brushing the ball or brushing the racket up behind the ball.

Generally speaking, when the ball is from waist high up to the shoulder, the racket-face is at the moment of impact vertical, and thus engages the ball, hitting it a smart blow and sending it on its way with a large amount of top spin on it, which is an invaluable quality in a passing shot.

It is of importance to remember that in making this

Plate 22.

THE BACKHAND DRIVE.

This is what happens if the thumb is left below the handle and the
forearm is not allowed to turn naturally. The player becomes
"locked on the shoulder" and the finish of the stroke is quite
ruined. Players who finish thus never get "top" on their ball.
This finish is a clear indication that the stroke was badly played.

stroke, or any other stroke in the game, it is advisable always when one can do so to take a short step with the foot at the moment one is hitting the ball. On the forehand the step will be taken with the left foot; on the backhand, with the right foot, and in all cases it should be the endeavor of the player so to judge the distance from the ball that this short step will put him into the correct position for striking it.

A player should always aim at acquiring certainty in playing balls without putting any spin on them. After he has done this he may begin to study the intricacies of the various spins, which now play such an important part in modern Tennis, although in 1904, when these things were fully explained, English players scoffed, because they did not understand them, and, on account of their faulty grip of the racket, could not do them. Their lack of initiative and their wrong principles have cost them their place in the game. They will never regain it until they return to the grips shown in this book.

Plate 23.

THE BACKHAND DRIVE.

This plate shows the finish of the backhand drive. Note carefully that the weight has gone on to the right foot, and that the arm has turned over until the thumb shows *above* the handle instead of *below* it.

The Backhand Stroke

This stroke is usually made in very bad form. The position of the feet is at all times a matter of very great importance, but it is especially so in the production of the backhand stroke.

The player, at the time of striking the ball, should have the right foot turned toward the net. This gives him the opportunity of bending his body sideways when he swings back with his racket, so that the racket swings underneath his body, and the player also has every opportunity to get to the back of the swing, whereas, if he were to face the net, his arm would come across his chest and his stroke would thus be interfered with.

The right foot is generally pointing almost where the ball is meant to be driven to, for in all drives in tennis the finish should be so that the weight of the player's body goes in a line down his front foot; in fact, the finish of any stroke in tennis should throw the player into the position in which he desires to be in order to start a run. This, of course, one would not be if one played across one's feet.

In the backhand stroke, the ball is taken farther from the player's body than is the case in the forehand drive.

The reason for this will be apparent from a study of

Plate 24.

THE BACKHAND DRIVE.

This shows a good finish of a backhand drive. The weight has gone on to the right foot and the follow-through is quite free and natural. Observe how the thumb has come up *above* the handle of the racket from its position at impact behind or below it. The wrist must be like steel at the finish, and it is indeed as firm as a rock throughout the stroke.

the photographs. It is very rare, indeed, to find a tennis player with a good backhand drive.

There is no reason whatever why players should not cultivate this stroke and I am certain that anyone carefully following out the instructions given, can acquire this most beautiful and effective shot.

There is only one man in America who can be said to really drive the ball on the backhand. The reason for this is that many of the players here have followed the English idea of holding the racket off the line of the arm. The moment this is done the racket becomes an excrescence on the side of the arm, instead of being, as it should, a continuation of the arm.

The Single Game

First, of all, cultivate accuracy. After that one may begin to improve one's pace. Length and accuracy are the two things which a singles player wants and after one has got these one has the right to begin practising for speed.

It is a great mistake to be too anxious to win off every stroke. One should endeavor always to play one's stroke so that if one cannot beat one's opponent outright, one at least makes him play his stroke so that he is at a disadvantage.

It is a great mistake to think that one's returns should just skim the net. If one plays for this, one will very quickly see a large number of them go into the net. One should keep firmly in one's mind that, especially with the forehand lifting drive, it is possible to drive two feet above the net and get a good length fast return.

The Return of the Service

The two returns which are generally used are a cross-court shot or a side-line drive. Especially in doubles, it is useful to understand the value of service down the centre of the court. This delivery cuts out the side-line shot down what is commonly called the alley and there is considerably less of the angle of the ordinary cross-court shot left to one's opponent.

The Double Game

There are four methods of returning the service in the double game, viz.: the Side-line Drive, the Cross-court Drive, the Centre Drive and the Lob.

The centre drive is perhaps the best return in doubles and it is most certainly the safest, because there is often some doubt as to who should volley the return of the service and frequently the ball is inadvertently left; off this return the ball is frequently volleyed when it would have gone out if not played.

The side-line drive is made so that the ball travels almost parallel with the side line.

It is a good idea to use this drive occasionally, as it prevents the man at the net from getting over too much to the centre of the court, and so cutting off the cross-court return or centre drive. A clean drive down the side line will tell him that he must remain at home.

Synopsis of the Laws of the Game

The balls which are played with are not to be less than 2½ inches, nor more than 2 9/16 inches in diameter and not less than 1 15/16 ounces nor more than 2 ounces in weight.

It is usual to toss to decide who shall serve first or who shall have the choice of the courts. Generally the racket is tossed and "rough" or "smooth" is called. The "rough" side of the racket is where the small colored cross strings at each end do not run across in a straight line, but are shown coiled around the gut. "Smooth" is the side of the racket where this stringing apparently runs in an unbroken line from side to side.

The player who wins the toss has the right to say whether he will take the choice of sides or the service. This is a matter which is sometimes of considerable importance in matches, having regard to sun or wind.

In serving the player must stand with both feet behind, that is, farther from the net than the base line, and within the limits of the imaginary continuation of the centre service and the side lines.

He must stand still before he begins to serve. That is, he may not walk up and serve without stopping, nor may he have both feet off the ground at or immediately before the moment of striking the ball, nor is he permitted to pass one foot over the line at or immediately before the moment of striking the ball, even if that foot is in the air and does not come down in the court.

He must not have one or both feet on the base line at the moment of serving. He must place both feet on the ground immediately before serving and must not take a running or walking start.

He must serve from the right and left courts alternately.

The ball must drop into the "Service Court," which is diagonally opposite to the half court from which it is served.

It is a good service if the ball drops on any line bounding the service court.

It is a fault if the service is delivered from the wrong court or if the server does not stand as already indicated, or if the ball served drops in the net or outside the service court diagonally opposite as aforesaid.

If the server misses the ball altogether it does not count as a fault, but if the ball be touched, no matter how lightly, by the racket, the service is thereby delivered and the laws governing the service at once apply.

The receiver may not take a fault.

If the server has made a fault, he should serve again from the court from which he served the fault, unless it was a fault because it was served from the wrong court.

It is **not** permitted to hit the service before it has struck the ground, but it must strike the ground in the service court for which it is intended before it can be played.

The ball is in play from the moment at which it is delivered in service (unless a fault), until it has been volleyed by the receiver in his first stroke, or has dropped in the net or out of the court, or has touched one of the players or anything that he wears or carries, except his racket in the act of striking, or has been struck by either of the players more than once consecutively, or has been volleyed before it has passed over the net, or has failed to pass over the net before its first bound, or has touched the ground twice consecutively on either side of the net, although the second time may be out of court.

It is a let if the ball in service touches the net, provided the service is otherwise good. In this case the **stroke** is played over again without loss to either player.

Either player loses a stroke if the ball touches him or anything that he wears or carries, except his racket in the act of striking, or if he volleys the ball, unless he thereby makes a good return, no matter whether he is standing within the limits of the court or outside; or if he touches or strikes the ball more than once consecutively, or if he or his racket (in his hand or otherwise) touches **the net** or any of its supports while the ball is in play, or if he volleys the ball before it has passed the net.

MAURICE E. McLOUGHLIN,
Conqueror of Norman E. Brookes and Anthony F. Wilding in Davis Cup singles.

Bundy and McLoughlin vs. Brookes and Wilding.
DAVIS CUP DOUBLES.

McLOUGHLIN VS. BROOKES—DAVIS CUP SINGLES.

Brown Bros., N. Y., Photo.

What is New in Tennis

Since the introduction some years ago of the Spalding Gold Medal rackets, originally made in two models, it has been our constant aim to improve and expand this special line of rackets to meet the demands and requirements of what we might call the composite experience of experts from all over the States, Europe and Australia.

Practically every reasonable requirement that can be looked for in a racket—stringing, distribution of weight, playing surface, grip, shape—is present in the one or the other of the Spalding Gold Medal models, and until now we felt sure we had the "last word" in racket manufacture.

We did not sit back and rest on our laurels, however, content with what we had accomplished, but, as has always been the Spalding custom, strove to excel ourselves, and, in the new Spalding "Autograph" racket we feel sure that we have succeeded in producing an implement that is unquestionably the finest ever made. Reinforced inside the depressed throat with selected rawhide, and outside from the shoulders down into the very handle itself, it minimizes to the smallest degree the possibility of a broken frame. The upper part of the frame is beautifully beveled, and the handle made entirely of cedar. The stringing is of the finest grade of lambs' gut, done by the most expert stringers in our shops. The racket is highly polished and finished in either brown or black. The brown style has brown throatpiece, brown rawhide reinforcement at shoulders and maroon trimming gut. All white stringing, in "expert" style. The black style has black throatpiece, black rawhide reinforcement at shoulders and black trimming gut. White vertical and black cross strings, in "expert" style. Handles are 5, 5¼ or 5⅜ inches in circumference. Price, including a waterproof cover, $10.00.

The "International" is the 1915 addition to our $8.00 Gold Medal models and rounds out the greatest line of high grade rackets ever offered to the public. Graceful lines, lots of playing surface and raised throatpiece, it gives the player confidence in his strokes as soon as he grasps it.

In addition to the "International," the line of $8.00 rackets includes such favorites as the Gold Medal No. GMB, All-Comers, Olympic, Model H, and the ever-popular "Hackett and Alexander," each with its own particular point of popularity. Excellent rackets, ones that were "championship" class only a few years ago, are Models GX, DH and EH, which sell at $5.00, while the "Tournament," at $4.00; the "Slocum," at $3.50; the Nassau and Lakeside, at $3.00; Oval, $2.50; Greenwood, $2.00; Geneva, $1.50, and Favorite, $1.25, are all representative of Spalding quality at their respective prices.

Speed on the court, ability to last, an all-around, well-balanced game are three qualities necessary to a good player. The Spalding Championship Ball has all these, and wherever it is used we are certain our judgment will be confirmed. Made in two weights of covers—No. OO for turf courts and No. OOH for hard courts. The latter ball has met with remarkable success on hard courts throughout the country, so much so that it is popularly known as the "Spalding Hard Court Ball," and was selected as the official ball of the Clay Court tournament of 1914, held at Cincinnati, and has been again officially adopted for the Clay Court championship of 1915, to be held this year on the courts of the Pittsburgh Athletic Association, June 26 and following days.

Incidentally, it may be mentioned that the challenge match of the Davis Cup tournament of 1914 was played over a Spalding No. 9-O championship net.

For clubs holding tournaments, many articles are now absolute necessities that were unknown a few years ago. While nets, posts, and all the direct paraphernalia of the game itself must be correct and in good shape, the umpire's chair and a scoring tree are just as much a part of the setting nowadays as seats for the spectators, and for clubs holding tournaments a "club" racket press is most essential.

To have a favorite racket put out of commission by some "chair caner" has more than once caused the loss of a match, as many players can testify. We make a specialty of restringing rackets, using the best of materials, and, what is even better, brains. Our stringers are men who are employed continually throughout the year, not for a few months in the season only—and coming in contact with the leading players, who naturally go to Spalding's for their requirements, these men are in an unequaled position to obtain at first hand all the little niceties of stringing that experience has shown to be most effective and which goes to make up that "just a bit better" that distinguishes the expert from the ordinary player. All of which is at the command of our patrons.

Several players who found the glare of a semi-tropic sun on Southern courts most trying during the past winter took a leaf out of the base ball player's notebook and used a form of sun-glass invented by Manager Fred Clarke of the Pittsburgh National League base ball club for the use of outfielders. The arrangement, which is fastened to the player's cap or hat, is substantial but not cumbersome, and has a hinged attachment which permits the glasses to be turned up out of the way when not needed. They cost $10.

Another novelty is an improvement over the regulation sweatband. It consists of a sweatband and visor—or sunshade—combined and sells for 75 cents.

Probably next to the racket a player's shoes are the most important part of his equipment, and necessarily so, for an ill-fitting pair is a handicap right from the start. A style that has found favor with many prominent players is the Spalding No. BBH, which is ideal for tournament play on turf courts, and fitted with officially approved blunt spikes in soles and heels. It is high cut, with finest quality kangaroo uppers, white oak soles and spring heels, and sells for $6.00 per pair.

For clay court use, No. AB is the most desirable style. It laces all the way down to the toe, being just high enough to give support to the ankle and yet not bind too tightly. High cut, drab calf, Blucher style, with heavy red rubber suction soles. No. AB costs $5.00 per pair.

A canvas shoe much favored by players who desire something stronger than the ordinary type of "sneaker" for clay courts is the Spalding No. HH, which is really a high "sneaker" with an extra heavy sole of best quality rubber. No. HH costs $2.25 per pair, and low cut, of same quality—when it is known as No. H—costs $2.00 per pair.

In this connection it is well to call attention to the fact that we also resole rubber soled shoes of our own make, the work being done in the Spalding shoe factory where the shoes are made. This is a convenience that is obvious, and one that other dealers are unable to offer.

Tennis players who contemplate being present—either as contestants or spectators—at the clay court championships at Pittsburgh in June, or the National Championships, to be held this year on the courts of the West Side Tennis Club, at Forest Hills, Long Island, in August, are invited to make use of the Spalding stores in both Pittsburgh and New York as their headquarters. A corps of specially selected stringers will be on hand and no effort will be spared to make Spalding service coequal with Spalding quality.

www.ingramcontent.com/pod-product-compliance
Lightning Source LLC
Chambersburg PA
CBHW050610160726
48003CB00003B/1124